This book belongs to the nicest child in the whole world:

# Lotsa de Casha

BY

MADONNA

ART BY

RUI PAES

CALLAWAY
NEW YORK
2005

To my husband,
who gives me lotsa everything.

Long, long ago and quite a distance away, there lived a very rich merchant who went by the name of Lotsa de Casha.

Lotsa was by far the richest man in the country. He had everything that money could buy. But there was a teeny, tiny problem. No matter how much money Lotsa de Casha made, he wasn't happy. No matter how many grand castles, fast horses, or fancy carriages he bought, he was still a gloomy old sourpuss.

One day, when Lotsa could not take being unhappy for one more second, he cried out, “Enougha is enougha. I can’ta take it anymore!”

You see, deep down inside, Lotsa was a good person. But being happy remained a complete mystery to him, and he knew he had to do something about it.

So he decided to speak to the very best doctors that money could buy. Every day he set out in one of his fancy carriages, and every day he returned without an answer. It soon became obvious that none of the doctors could help him with his problem.

Now, Lotsa's driver, who saw how unhappy his boss was, decided to tell him about a wise old man who lived miles and miles away in the ancient city. "I hear he has an answer for everything. Perhaps he will know how to help you, sir."

To this, Lotsa replied, "When I wanta your opinion, I'lla buy it from you."

Of course, Lotsa's driver was not offended, for he (like everyone else) had grown accustomed to Lotsa being difficult and impossible to please.

VRBS · ANTIQVA ·

In any case, Lotsa was so desperate that, without apologizing for being rude, he ordered his driver to take him to see the wise old man immediately.

He set off with his brightest carriage, his fastest horses, and his biggest sandwiches to see the wise old man who lived so far away.

After ten long days and nine long nights, Lotsa de Casha arrived at the ancient city.

There were many beautiful sights to see,
but to Lotsa's disappointment, his driver never stopped at any of them.
They drove past many great buildings
and cathedrals,
but
Lotsa was not impressed.
He was too busy feeling sorry for himself, since he had eaten all his sandwiches
and his tummy was growling.

Finally,
when Lotsa thought he would faint from hunger, his coach stopped outside
a dusty little hovel.
“What’sa thisa?” shouted Lotsa de Casha to his driver. “This is the address I was given, sir.”
“Thisa doesn’t look like the house of an important man to me,” said Lotsa. “Get outa and check.”
And so his driver did,
and sure enough, they had found
the right house.

Lotsa de Casha got out of the carriage, looked around to make sure that no one would see him, and banged on the door. The door opened, and there stood a little old man whose beard nearly touched the floor.

Lotsa introduced himself, and when the old man heard how far he had traveled, he insisted that Lotsa join him for lunch and tell him all about his problem.

"Goody, I'ma starving. I could eata a horse," said Lotsa, who was used to being waited on.

"We will not be eating one of those," said the wise man, with a hint of a grin. "But my wife is a great cook. Come into our kitchen and eat with us."

So they sat down at the tiny table, and Lotsa ate as if he hadn't eaten in weeks.

"It's a bada situation," Lotsa explained, after he had finished quite a delicious bowl of spaghetti.

"I have spent alla my lifea making da money, so I could be happy. Now I have alla da money a man could want, but still I'ma not happy."

The old man was not surprised in the least. He leaned closer to Lotsa and said, "There is a very important secret to be learned in life, but it's very hard to see, and even harder to hear, so most people miss it."

"What isa thata secret?" asked Lotsa, eager to hear the answer.

"The secret . . ." said the wise man, pausing for a second, while Lotsa sat up straight and strained to hear. "The secret is this: if you share what you have and put others before you, you will find happiness."

Lotsa de Casha was stumped. "Isa thata it?" he demanded.

"That'sa it," answered the old man.

Lotsa had never thought about sharing or putting others first. All his life, he had been told that if he wanted to become rich and successful, he had to think about only one thing: himself! He scratched his head and frowned. This couldn't be right. The old man was obviously a phony baloney. An impostor. A quack! Lotsa wanted to leave immediately.

"You must be a very busy man. Don't let me take up any more of your time," said Lotsa, pretending to be polite.

"As you wish," said the old man, smiling. "I hope you find what you are looking for."

"Thank you," snorted Lotsa, and he quickly walked to the door and slammed it behind him.

DOMUS
CONCORDIAE

Lotsa stood outside on the street for several minutes, not knowing what to do. The situation seemed rather hopeless. He had traveled so far, only to find out that the wise old man was a nutcase.

Lotsa decided he didn't want to talk to anyone for a while, not even his coach driver. He checked to make sure he had his big fat purse full of money and told the driver to stay put.

He needed to go for a walk.

He wanted to think.

He walked for hours and hours around the ancient city. After a while, he passed a man trying to change the wheel on his cart. The man looked up and caught his eye. It made Lotsa feel uneasy. It looked like the man had been working for hours, and he obviously needed help, but the job was messy and complicated. Besides, nobody else had bothered to stop and help. So why should Lotsa? He carried on with his walk and went back to thinking about himself and how he was going to find happiness.

Time passed, and Lotsa realized that it was getting dark, and there weren't any people on the streets. He didn't know where he was, or how to get back to his coach and driver.

Just then, two men came out of the shadows. One of them wore a patch over his eye and walked with a stick. The other was short and had no teeth.

They cried out to Lotsa, "Please help us, sir. We've fallen on hard times. Could you spare some change?"

"Certainly nota," said Lotsa, sniffing the air and wrinkling up his nose. "If you needa money, go and earn it." And with that, Lotsa turned to go.

Suddenly, the two men snarled and narrowed their eyes. The short one had a very menacing voice. "There must be a misunderstanding. We ain't asking you for yer money. We're taking it, yer Lordship."

The man with the patch on his eye started waving his stick around and shouting at Lotsa. "Let's have your clothes as well, Mr. Fancy Boots. And be quick about it."

No one had ever threatened Lotsa before. For the first time in his life he felt scared. He quickly gave them everything they wanted, and the two men ran off into the night, congratulating each other on a job well done.

Lotsa was left standing in his underpants and socks in the middle of a dark and lonely street. He could feel the sting of tears on his face. "Now, look at the mess I'ma in," he muttered to himself.

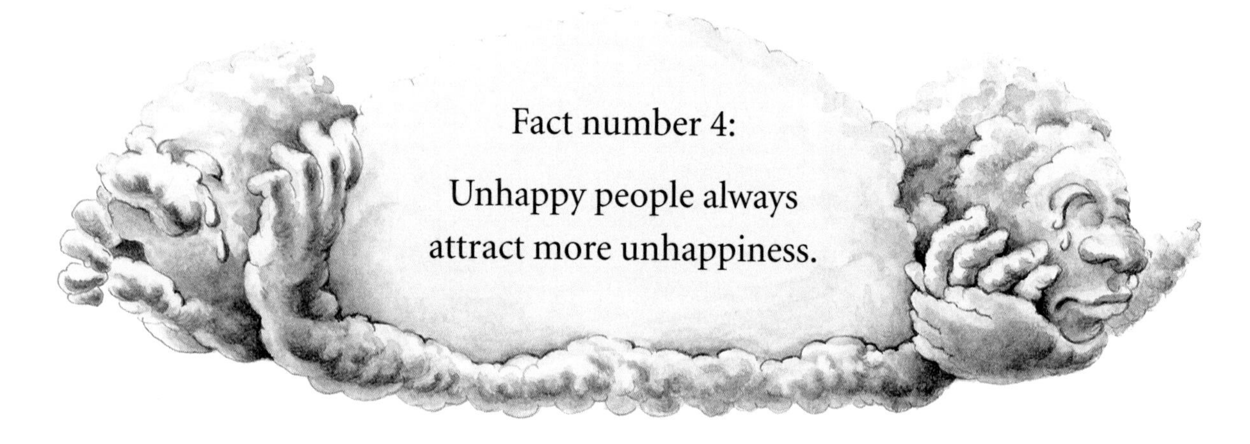


Suddenly, he heard the noise of a horse-drawn cart plodding down the street.

"Help! Help!" shouted Lotsa, as he ran to stop the cart.

"What are you doing standing in the middle of the street with no clothes on?" asked the rough-looking man driving the cart.

"I wasa robbed. Thieves came and beat me. They took everything. Please helpa me," cried Lotsa, feeling terribly humiliated.

"Did you help me when I needed it?" asked the man.

Then Lotsa realized it was the same man who had needed help changing the wheel of his cart—the same man Lotsa had ignored.

"I'ma so sorry," said Lotsa, instantly regretting that he hadn't helped him when he had been given the chance. Lotsa just stood there, whimpering in his underpants.

"Which way are you going?" asked the man.

"I want to go to my castle, Flasha de Casa," replied Lotsa. "It'sa at the foot of the Muchadougha Mountains."

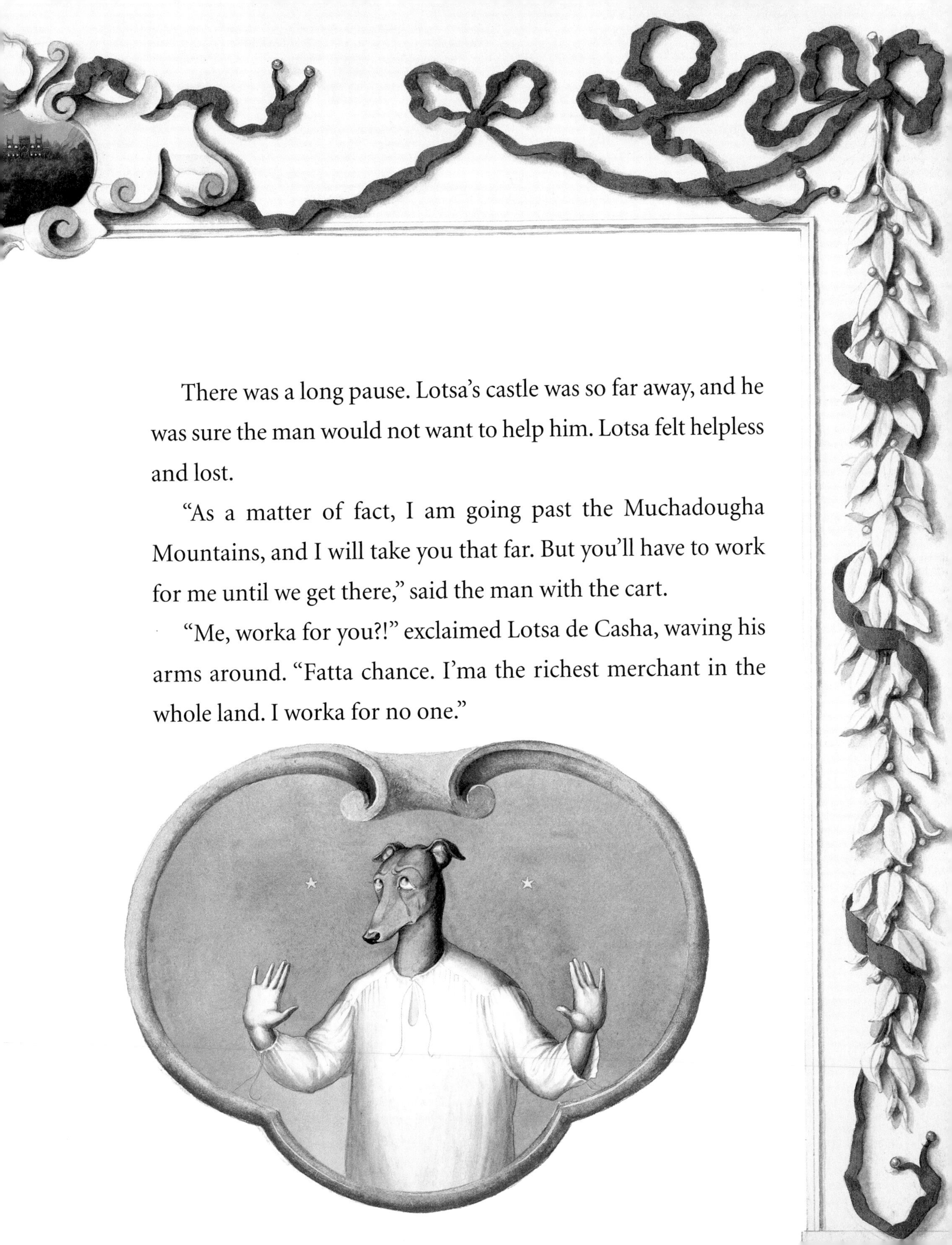

There was a long pause. Lotsa's castle was so far away, and he was sure the man would not want to help him. Lotsa felt helpless and lost.

"As a matter of fact, I am going past the Muchadougha Mountains, and I will take you that far. But you'll have to work for me until we get there," said the man with the cart.

"Me, worka for you?!" exclaimed Lotsa de Casha, waving his arms around. "Fatta chance. I'ma the richest merchant in the whole land. I worka for no one."

"All the money in the world won't help you now. Good luck," said the man as he started to ride away.

Lotsa began to panic. He knew he had no other choice. "Please come backa. I'ma sorry I offended you. Of course, I will worka for you."

"Well, hop on then," said the man. "And no complaining."

"No complaining," echoed Lotsa, struggling to climb aboard in his stocking feet.

"The name is Forfilla," announced the man, as he signaled his horse to move on. "But it's Mr. Forfilla to you."

"I'ma Lotsa de Casha—very happy to makea your acquaintance, Mr. Forfilla, sir," said Lotsa, wiping the tears from his eyes.

"Put this on. You look ridiculous," said Mr. Forfilla, giving Lotsa a warm blanket to wrap around himself.

When they got to the outskirts of town, they stopped outside a small shop. Mr. Forfilla asked Lotsa to bring a wooden desk from the back of his cart into the shop and give it to the man who was working there.

Lotsa felt a little silly because he wasn't wearing much more than a blanket. But he remembered the promise he had made and did as he was told.

It was a very heavy desk. Lotsa struggled to carry it on his own from the cart and through the door. It was a difficult job, and Lotsa was sweating by the time he returned to the cart.

Just as they were about to continue their journey, a little man came running out of the shop and kissed Mr. Forfilla's hand. He then handed him a pair of beautifully made boots.

When the man went back inside, Mr. Forfilla turned to Lotsa and said, "Put these on. You can't run errands for me in your stocking feet."

"These are the finesta boots I have ever seen," said Lotsa, feeling grateful for the first time in his life.

He put the boots on, and they fit perfectly. He wrapped himself in his blanket, and they continued on their journey.

Lotsa was very tired, and in a matter of minutes, he had fallen asleep.

When he woke up, it was morning. The sun was shining, the birds were singing, but the cart was not moving.

Mr. Forfilla was finishing off his breakfast. He looked at Lotsa and said, "Rise and shine, Mr. de Casha. In the back of the cart you will find an old chair. I want you to deliver it to the man who works inside that shop over there."

Lotsa wasn't too happy about having to work before breakfast, but he had made a promise to Mr. Forfilla, and he wanted to get home. So down he jumped in his new boots and, with his blanket wrapped around him, he picked up the chair from the back of the cart. In the daylight he noticed that this wasn't a normal, everyday chair. It was one of the finest chairs that money could buy and had been made with unbelievable love and care.

"This musta be worth a fortune!" exclaimed Lotsa.

Mr. Forfilla told Lotsa to stop talking and carry on with his job.

Lotsa carried the chair into the little shop. He could tell it was a tailor's shop because of all the clothes and equipment lying around. There, behind a desk, in a very uncomfortable chair, sat a very old man.

"Put it down there," said Mr. Forfilla, who had walked in behind Lotsa.

"Thank you. You are an angel," said the tailor to Mr. Forfilla. "My aching back will appreciate this great gift."

Then he dug under his desk and pulled out two very neatly folded jackets. "Please take these. They should keep you and your friend warm on a cold and windy night."

The tailor handed over the two magnificent jackets, which were made from the finest leather and sewn with the greatest of care.

Lotsa de Casha was speechless. It was the nicest gift he had ever received.

The next ten days continued in the same way. Mr. Forfilla would produce an assortment of things from the back of his wagon (hammers, paintings, blankets, and an endless supply of furniture and clothing), and Lotsa would carry them into people's homes and shops.

He had never worked so hard in his life. He had never seen so many people smile. He was starting to feel good about himself.

Every time Lotsa brought somebody something, he would receive something equally useful in return. And at the end of every day, a kind stranger would offer him and Mr. Forfilla a meal and a warm bed to sleep in.

Sometimes there was music,
and they would sing and dance.
Lotsa was sleeping better than
he could ever remember.

When they had almost reached their destination, Lotsa turned to Mr. Forfilla and said, "Your lifea isa so simple, and yet I can see you are a very happy man. How can thata be?"

Mr. Forfilla's face lit up, and his eyes glowed as if there were a large family of candles hiding behind them. "I am happy because I know a secret," he replied.

"And what isa thata secret?" asked Lotsa.

"It's really quite simple," said Mr. Forfilla. "If you share what you have and put others before you, you will find happiness."

Lotsa was stunned into silence, for this was the very same thing the old man in the ancient city had told him. But still, he felt confused.

They had been riding for hours through a forest, and Lotsa decided to take the reins and drive for a while, so that Mr. Forfilla could rest.

He wrapped the jacket he loved so much around himself, and while Mr. Forfilla slept, he thought about how lucky he was to have this great warm coat on such a cold and windy night.

He thought about how nice everyone had been. He realized that he hadn't thought about how much money he had for over a week. He realized he was happy.

When they reached the edge of the forest, they passed a shivering and barefoot beggar who didn't have a coat or boots to keep him warm. Lotsa felt sorry for him, but he kept on moving.

When he was halfway down the road, he stopped suddenly. All at once, he understood what everyone had been telling him. He now had the opportunity to put someone else's needs before his own.

He got off the cart and ran back to the beggar. He gave him his jacket and his boots and a big hug and a kiss.

"Please takea these! It would makea me so happy!" he exclaimed. Before the beggar could say thank you, Lotsa ran back to the cart.

As the sun was rising, Mr. Forfilla woke up and saw that Lotsa had the old blanket wrapped around himself and only a pair of socks on his feet.

"What happened to your clothes?" he asked.

Lotsa didn't say a thing. Instead, he turned to Mr. Forfilla and smiled for the first time since he was a child. His face lit up, and his eyes glowed as if there were a large family of candles hiding behind them. Mr. Forfilla knew exactly what had happened.

"We are now at the foot of the Muchadougha Mountains, and I can see your castle from here," said Mr. Forfilla.

"How do you know thata isa my castle?" asked Lotsa.

"Because it used to be mine, before you bought it," replied Mr. Forfilla. "You see, I was once a very rich man, and I lived all alone in that big castle. But I wasn't happy, until I came down off my high horse and shared what I had with others."

Lotsa was in shock. He was starting to see things for what they were.

"So that'sa where you gota all those fancy chairs!" he exclaimed.

"You're pretty smart for a guy with such a silly name," said Mr. Forfilla.

Lotsa threw his head back and laughed. He knew he had learned a very important secret about being happy.

Finally, they arrived at Flasha de Casa, and Lotsa jumped down from the cart.

"Come inside, and I'lla make you a sandwich," said Lotsa.

"I don't mind if I do," said Mr. Forfilla.

And the two friends made their way inside the castle.

Fact number 6:

When you learn to share, you will<br>not only find happiness.<br>You will also find a friend.

The End